After.

by Chad Beckim

A SAMUEL FRENCH ACTING EDITION

SAMUEL FRENCH

FOUNDED 1830

SAMUELFRENCH.COM

ISBN 978-0-573-70048-4   Printed in U.S.A.   #20250

MUSIC USE NOTE

Licensees are solely responsible for obtaining formal written permission from copyright owners to use copyrighted music in the performance of this play and are strongly cautioned to do so. If no such permission is obtained by the licensee, then the licensee must use only original music that the licensee owns and controls. Licensees are solely responsible and liable for all music clearances and shall indemnify the copyright owners of the play and their licensing agent, Samuel French, Inc., against any costs, expenses, losses and liabilities arising from the use of music by licensees.

IMPORTANT BILLING AND CREDIT
REQUIREMENTS

All producers of *AFTER.* *must* give credit to the Author of the Play in all programs distributed in connection with performances of the Play, and in all instances in which the title of the Play appears for the purposes of advertising, publicizing or otherwise exploiting the Play and/or a production. The name of the Author *must* appear on a separate line on which no other name appears, immediately following the title and *must* appear in size of type not less than fifty percent of the size of the title type.

In addition the following credit *must* be given in all programs and publicity information distributed in association with this piece:

After. **was developed, in part,**
with assistance from The Orchard Project,
a program of The Exchange.

After. **was originally produced by**
Partial Comfort Productions, NYC

AFTER. was first produced by the Partial Comfort Productions at The Wild Project in New York, New York in September 2011. The performance was directed by Stephen Brackett, with casting by Judy Bowman, set design by Jason Simms, costume design by Whitney Locher, lighting design by Greg Goff, sound design by Daniel Kluger, and dramaturgy by John M. Baker. The production manager was Lindsay Austen, the technical director was Derek Dickinson, the stage manager was Tara M. Nachtigall, the assistant manager was Hillary Poirier, and the fight director was David Anzuelo. Production interns were Emilia Aghamirzai, Lydian Blossom, and Jennifer Gomez. The cast was as follows:

SUSIE.	Jackie Chung
CHAP.	Andrew Garman
MONTY.	Alfredo Narciso
LIZ	Maria-Christina Oliveras
WARREN	Debargo Sanyal
EDDIE	Jeff Wilburn

CHARACTERS

MONTY - Latino, mid-30's
LIZ - Monty's sister, early-30's
CHAP - Any ethnicity, 40's - 50's
WARREN - Indian, early-30's
SUSIE - Asian, early-30's
MAN/EDDIE - Latin, mid-to-late 30's

Scene 1

(Late night. A small dining room. The aftermath of a large meal: empty plates, glasses, crumpled napkins. A "Welcome Home" banner hangs over the table.)

*(***MONTY*** *paces in front of the dining room window. One-two three-four-five-six. Stop. Peek through the space between the shade and the window. Repeat. He does this for a long, long while [at least thirty seconds real time]. Silence, except for the creaks of the floor and the scuff of his feet on the carpet, then:)*

*(***LIZ*** *enters, pausing as she watches* ***MONTY*** *pace, unaware that she's there.)*

LIZ. Monty?

MONTY. Huh?

LIZ. What's wrong?

MONTY. Huh? Nothing.
Did I wake you? I'm
sorry, I didn't mean
to wake you.   **LIZ**. You didn't. I wanted a
                                glass of water.

                                Why are you down here?

MONTY. I wanted a glass of water. Too.

LIZ. Oh. *(short beat, realization)* Shit. I didn't even clean the table.

MONTY. Leave it til tomorrow.

LIZ. I don't want mice.

(She begins stacking dishes.)

MONTY. We have mice?

LIZ. Not if we clean the table, we don't.

(Silence. She stacks dishes. He studies the room: the walls, the floors, the photos and decor.)

LIZ. How was dinner? Was it good? Did you like it? I tried thinking of everything you might like to eat and figured I'd go old school. I saw this other thing on a cooking show and was gonna try it, but—

MONTY. It was great, Liz. Thank you.

LIZ. I'm sorry I feel
asleep so early. I'm –
– so tired.   MONTY. It's okay.

LIZ. Still. I wanted to hang out. I didn't mean to fall asleep on you. I went up to change, and boom, I knocked out. I woke up, my back on the bed, my feet touching the floor. *(short beat)* Why are you in the dining room? You hungry?

MONTY. I wanted to look out the window.

LIZ. Oh. Okay. I mean, you're not tired?

MONTY. No.

LIZ. I figured you'd be knocked out. Long day, today. A good day.

(She exits with a stack of dishes.)

LIZ. *(offstage)* Tomorrow, maybe we could go into the city, get you some new clothes. Maybe some groceries? I thought we'd have more time today, but...

MONTY. What day is tomorrow?

(She reenters.)

LIZ. Wednesday. Kevin gave me the day off – isn't even counting it against my vacation. I thought that maybe we could go somewhere. Maybe shopping, or to the water, or to the movies, maybe? Or get a massage? The *chinitas* have a new place up the block, $35 a person.

MONTY. I have some interviews tomorrow.

LIZ. Already? Great. Well then, maybe I'll go to the massage.

MONTY. Maybe after? Or maybe I can rearrange it?

LIZ. No, don't do that. I'm teasing you. We'll see how you feel. Okay? Okay.

(A short beat. Silence. MONTY walks to the entrance, stares down the hallway.)

LIZ. *(offstage)* Is your room okay? I set it up all nice for you. New sheets, new pillows.

MONTY. It's fine, Liz.

LIZ. *(offstage)* And I wasn't sure what to do, but I took the posters down. If you want them back up, they're rolled up in the closet with an elastic, but –

(She reenters.)

– I figured you'd probably want them down. I don't even know if "Smashing Pumpkins" is still around any more. And Kurt Cobain. There was another one taped in half from where Papi ripped it, but I couldn't -

(She stacks the few remaining dishes.)

MONTY. Where do you sleep?

LIZ. What?

MONTY. Where do you sleep? Your room is an office.

(She sets the dishes down. MONTY turns.)

LIZ. I sleep in the big bedroom.

MONTY. Mami and Papi's old room?

LIZ. ...Yes.

MONTY. Huh.

(She exits with the remaining dishes. MONTY turns back towards the hallway.)

LIZ. *(offstage)* Oh!

(She reenters, holding an envelope.)

Oh! This came for you.

(MONTY turns, regards her. She hands him the envelope.)

There's no return address, but -

MONTY. Thank you.

(He sits at the table, staring at the envelope.)

(She begins wiping down the table, watching him, expectantly.)

LIZ. Surprise mail is always exciting. You going to open it?

(He drops the envelope on the table.)

MONTY. No.

LIZ. Okay then.

(A short beat. Silence.)

LIZ. It's quiet, huh?

MONTY. Yes.

LIZ. You want something to drink? Some tea, maybe?

MONTY. I'm okay.

LIZ. Are you sure? *(She turns to exit.)* Let me make you some tea. I bought this kind called "Sleepytime," and—   **MONTY**. No. No, Liz. It's okay.

LIZ. You sure I can't get you something? Anything?

MONTY. It's okay. Go back to bed.

(She finishes, yawns, stretches. She begins to exit, glances over her shoulder, and stops, staring at him.)

MONTY. What?

(She snaps out of it, smiles.)

LIZ. Nothing. Welcome Home.

*(She smiles at him, pauses, then exits. He stares down the hall for a few seconds, waiting. A beat. **MONTY** opens the envelope and glances inside, then rips it in half. He rises and begins pacing again. One two-three-four-five-six...)*

Scene 2

(One week later. **CHAP** *and* **LIZ** *in the dining room.*
CHAP *sits, mug in hand.* **LIZ** *stands, also holding a
mug.)*

LIZ. And then you drop your coffee into the water and stir
it in and lower the temperature to a medium high.
You let that cook for one minute, then shut off the
heat and add a cover for one more minute.

And then you're going
to put the strainer -
El Colador - it kind of
looks like a sock on a
handle?

You   pour   your   **CHAP**. It sounds like a bull-
coffee—   fighter.

LIZ. Huh?

CHAP. *El Colador?* It sounds like a bullfighter.

*(**LIZ** laughs, maybe a little too hard.)*

LIZ. Ha! Yes, it does. That's funny. That's so funny.

CHAP. ...

LIZ. Oh! So next you pour your coffee mixture through *el
colador* into the cup.

Then you rinse the saucepan out and put the flame
on medium high, and you pour in your milk – I use
whole milk, even though it's more old school to use
Condensed Milk. I find it hurts my teeth, so I use
whole milk, and add sugar. I like one spoon, but some
people like more or less, you know? Anyways, once
it starts to foam up on the sides of the pan, you pour
your coffee back into it and let that cook on medium.

When it comes to a boil, you lower *your* flame and let
it cook for another minute or so. And then you pour
your coffee back into your cup, and voila!

Cafe con Leche. Just like Mami used to make.

CHAP. Well, this is quite wonderful.

LIZ. I'm glad you like it. I can write down the recipe for you.

CHAP. I will certainly be focused on my drive home.

LIZ. …

CHAP. The caffeine? I'm usually a tea drinker.

LIZ. Oh. I can make you tea, if you want! Let me make you some tea!   **CHAP**. No, please, this is lovely. Really.

(a short beat)

CHAP. Do you have any idea when he might be back?

LIZ. He should be here anytime. He just went to the store.

(a short beat)

It's nice to finally meet you, Father.

All this time and we've   **CHAP**. Please, call me Chap. never—   Everyone calls me Chap.

LIZ. Oh. Right. Chap. Sorry. I should know better. You're not wearing—

(She points to her neck.)

CHAP. I'm not here in any official capacity.

LIZ. Oh. You're not? Okay.

CHAP. So how is he doing?

(a short beat)

LIZ. Fine. I think he's fine.

CHAP. That's good to hear.

LIZ. *I'm* mostly guessing, because he doesn't talk a lot. Also he doesn't really eat a lot?

And he never sleeps. He paces all night. He doesn't think that I know, but I know.

CHAP. Out here. Am I right?

LIZ. Yes, how did you -

CHAP. Biggest window in the house. That's normal.

LIZ. I know it's only been a couple of days, but. This is just. A lot, you know? And. I'm not really used to having anyone here, so there's that. Does everything look okay?

CHAP. How do you mean?

LIZ. You know, everything here. Does it look okay, his room and the house and everything?

CHAP. Everything looks fine.

LIZ. If there's anything you can think of – ? I tried googling it, like "What to expect?" but there's nothing. Not for this situation, anyways. And it's just me, here? I don't know what I'm supposed to do. Like, am I supposed to try to talk about any of it? Do I ask him questions? Do I help him with stuff? Or leave him be? Do I... – ?

*(**MONTY** enters behind her. **CHAP** rises. **MONTY** stares at **CHAP**. **LIZ** turns, sees **MONTY**.)*

LIZ. Hi, Monty!

CHAP. Hello, Monty.

MONTY. What are you doing here?

CHAP. I was in the neighborhood.

MONTY. You hang out in Sunnyside, now?

LIZ. Okay. I'm gonna just go in the other room. Can I get either of you anything?

MONTY. No.   **CHAP**. No, thank you.

LIZ. *(to **CHAP**)* Will I see you before you leave?

CHAP. I'll make it a point to say goodbye.

LIZ. Okay! Oh – Monty – where did you put the laundry soap?

MONTY. ...I didn't get it. I forgot. I'm sorry.

LIZ. You – *(recovering)* Okay. I'll run out and get that. I'll be back in a little bit.

*(She exits. A beat. **CHAP** steps forward, hand extended. A half beat, then **MONTY** shakes it.)*

CHAP. I realize this visit is unexpected. I hope this isn't a problem.

MONTY. ...

CHAP. Your sister kept me company while I waited for you. It was nice to put a face with a name.

MONTY. ...What were you two talking about?

CHAP. *Cafe con Leche.* She gave me her recipe. *(a short beat)* Do you mind if we sit?

MONTY. ...Go ahead.

(*CHAP sits. A half beat, then MONTY sits. A long beat.*)

CHAP. So how is everything?

(*MONTY shrugs.*)

The food?

(*MONTY shrugs.*)

She tells me you haven't been eating much.

(*MONTY shrugs.*)

She said you're wearing out the carpet, as well.

(*MONTY immediately looks down.*)

There's a lot of room here, brother. Lots of room.

(*a short beat*)

MONTY. Why are you here again?

CHAP. I told you, I was in the neighborhood.   **MONTY**. In the neighborhood. Yeah, yeah, you said that.

CHAP. I was.

MONTY. You live ninety minutes upstate.

CHAP. All I did is drop in to say hello. I can go, if you'd like.

MONTY. No. You don't have to go. *(a short beat)* You do this with everyone? Or is this, you know, some kind of official check in?

CHAP. No. It's not an official check in. This isn't part of my job.

MONTY. But it's a check in.

CHAP. It's not a check in.

MONTY. What is it, then?

CHAP. I wanted to see how you were doing.

MONTY. A check in.

CHAP. A friendly chat. We're friends, right? And isn't that what friends do? Have friendly chats?

MONTY. I guess.

CHAP. Then that's why I'm here.

MONTY. As long as you don't expect me to say anything.

CHAP. No, I learned that lesson. Took me a number of years, but I learned it.

    *(**MONTY** smiles. A short beat.)*

MONTY. Do you ever talk to WoJo?

CHAP. Once in a while. If I see him around.

MONTY. If you could ask him, how's the puppy?

CHAP. Puppy? She's gotta be, what, six or seven by now?

MONTY. Seven. If you could find out? And if I could see her?

CHAP. I'll find out.

    (a short beat)

MONTY. Laura Miller sent me a letter.

CHAP. What did she say?

MONTY. Return to Sender.

CHAP. That's your prerogative, but you may want to consider talking to her at some point. Because – if I may – I think it's important that–

MONTY. Anything else? Any other paperwork or loose ends that they sent you to take care of? Because they already talked to me about the other thing, and I told them just get it over with.

    (a short beat)

CHAP. No one sent me here, Monty.

MONTY. …

CHAP. What's going on with you?

MONTY. It's just. You're watching me like Liz.

CHAP. How is that?

MONTY. Like, waiting. Expecting me to say something.

CHAP. How does that make you feel?

> (*Both men smile.* **MONTY** *gives* **CHAP** *the finger. A short beat.*)

CHAP. Have you asked her what she's expecting you to say?

MONTY. No.

CHAP. Maybe you should. Anything else?

MONTY. I'm tired.

CHAP. You're not sleeping?

MONTY. …Sleepwalking?

> (*a short beat*)

CHAP. You're sleepwalking?

MONTY. Yes. Does it mean something?

CHAP. It could. You tell me.

MONTY. I mean…uh…yeah… There's…you know.

> (**MONTY** *looks at the floor.*)

Before I went to sleep the other night - my first night, you know - I started thinking about…

How…just, you know…fucked. All of this is.

Just - just - just -

Everything.

Fucked.

I have nothing.

CHAP. You know that's not -

MONTY. No, it's the truth.

I have nothing.

No skills.

No job.

No family – I mean, there's my sister, but – yeah. No, whatever, wife or girlfriend or kids who were waiting for me –

no family of my own.

And I fell asleep. Thinking of that.

The nothingness.

(a short beat)

And I woke up, and – and – and–

I woke up and I'm in

my sister's car.

In the garage.

Behind the wheel.

And - and - and -

the engine is running.

And. It's. Just. Yeah. It's

hard to breathe.

And I wake up and. Yeah. I wake up and think *"Fuck it."*

CHAP. Monty.

(He leans forward, hand over his mouth. Silence. A short beat. MONTY smiles.)

MONTY. And I'm totally fucking with you right now. How does that make you feel?

(CHAP stares at him. Silence. He rises.)

CHAP. This was a mistake.

MONTY. I'm sorry.

CHAP. No, you're right. I shouldn't have come here. I didn't mean to waste your time. Or mine. There are actually people who want to talk to me.

CHAP. *(cont.)* Who need to
talk to me. I don't have
to come here. I prob-
ably shouldn't come
here. So I'm going
to go. Because this
is horse shit, Monty.   **MONTY.** I'm sorry. I
It's horse shit.   shouldn't–
                                        I'm sorry.

CHAP. *(cracking a smile)* And I'm totally fucking with you
right now.

*(They laugh. **CHAP** sips the coffee.)*

(re: coffee) This is terrible.

*(**MONTY** smiles. A short beat.)*

MONTY. Just now? Liz asked me to go to the store. It's nice
out. So I figured I would take a little walk. And I was
crossing–about to cross–the street. And the little 'walk'
guy comes on and I start to cross and I can't move.

I'm just.

Stuck.

Just...

There.

My legs won't move and the people behind me are
bumping into me and yelling at me and calling me
names but.

And then the light starts blinking red

and then the little hand comes on and.

I think, "If I run now, I can make it."

But I don't.

I.

Can't.

Stupid, you know?

I couldn't.

Can't.

Cross the street.

And this guy behind me yells, "Walk, you fucken' idiot!"

And I did.

And. Yeah.

I don't even know how to walk any more without some-one telling me.

(CHAP stares at MONTY, who looks up at him. A very long beat.)

MONTY. I wasn't joking that time.

CHAP. I know.

Scene 3

(The toothbrush section of a drugstore.)

*(**MONTY** stares at the toothbrushes.)*

(He stares some more.)

(He stares some more.)

*(**SUSIE** walks past the aisle. She backs up and watches him stare for a moment, then:)*

SUSIE. Hi there?

*(**MONTY** jumps.)*

I'm sorry-I didn't mean
to scare you.   **MONTY**. It's okay. You didn't.

SUSIE. Yes I did! But I'm used to it.

MONTY. You are?

SUSIE. Sure! I'm scary. Rahhhhhhh! *(short beat)* So - can I help you with something?

MONTY. I'm trying to pick out a toothbrush.

SUSIE. I know.

MONTY. You do?

SUSIE. Well, you've been standing in front of the tooth-brush section for 30 minutes. I walked by before and saw you.

MONTY. Oh. Yeah. It's hard.

SUSIE. It's just a toothbrush.

MONTY. You don't have the kind that I'm used to.

SUSIE. We don't? Really? Are you sure?

MONTY. I looked.

SUSIE. All of these toothbrushes and we don't have what you want?

MONTY. No.

SUSIE. Hmmmmm…because I thought we carried just about everything.

MONTY. Yeah. I looked, and you don't have it.

SUSIE. Well, what kind of toothbrush are you looking for?

MONTY. I… *(He turns back to the rack and studies them.)* I don't know. You don't have the one that I'm used to. There are too many to choose from, and–

SUSIE. Well, let's see if we can't find something equal or better, yeah? Okay. So. Soft, medium, or firm?

MONTY. Firm, I think?

SUSIE. Oh, that's bad. It's bad for your gums. Makes them recede. My dentist says you should go with the soft.

MONTY. Okay.

SUSIE. Now. What else… Okay, the head – tapered or rectangular? And then there's the bristles, rippled, flat, blah blah blah, the handle, electric or manual – huh. I guess there are a lot of options.

(She stares at him. A short beat.)

SUSIE. Okay…well, in that case, what color do you like?

MONTY. Uh…

SUSIE. Oh, come on, you! Everyone has a favorite color. Mine's green. What's yours?

MONTY. Green is nice.

SUSIE. Yay! Go green! So that narrows us down a lot, right? So. Soft bristled. Green.

(She grabs a brush off the rack.)

SUSIE. Is that okay?

MONTY. Yeah. That's fine. Thank you.

(He stares at the toothbrush. She stares at him, then hangs her head.)

SUSIE. I'm sorry.

MONTY. For what?

SUSIE. I do this all the time - it's a bad habit and I do it and I'm trying not to do it anymore but it's sort of ingrained, like this horrible part of my personality, I guess, but. Yeah. I'm sorry.

MONTY. I don't understand. What did you do?

(She gestures to the toothbrush.)

SUSIE. That.

MONTY. What? Helped me pick out a toothbrush?

SUSIE. No, I didn't help you, I forced it on you. I saw you
and wanted to be helpful and instead of being helpful and letting you choose the brush, I came over and
inserted myself and asserted myself and made an ass of
myself. I've been told that I have problems with that.
I've been told that I often confuse being helpful with
being assertive.

MONTY. Who told you that?

SUSIE. Noone. Nevermind.

(a short beat)

Can I help you with anything else?

MONTY. No. I mean, yes. Where's the deodorant aisle?

SUSIE. It's over there Two aisles down.

(She pulls away, studying him).

SUSIE. You're not one of those "Axe" guys, are you?

MONTY. What's an "Axe" guy?

SUSIE. You know - pssssssshhhhhhhhhhttttttttt!

*(She "sprays" herself. **MONTY** stares.)*

You've never seen it? "Axe?" It's this horribly smelly
shit that for some reason guys think smell good and
spray all over themselves. You don't look like an "Axe"
guy. Please don't be an "Axe" guy.

MONTY. I'm not an - "Axe" guy.

SUSIE. I don't get that, you know? Like, you'll see these
good looking guys, well groomed, well maintained,
together, the kind of guy that you see and secretly
think, "He looks like a nice guy to talk to," only then
they walk past you and they smell like they just got
stuck in a cologne thunderstorm. You're Latino, right?

(He nods.)

SUSIE. *(cont.)* And you don't stink like that. You smell natural. Like soap or something. Which is good. So what's up with that? I only ask because, it actually made me stop dating black and Latin guys. Which sucks, because I actually prefer black and Latin guys. White guys are too boring and Asian guys have mom issues. And Jews.

(She hangs her head again.)

That wasn't racist, was it? I'm sorry. I'm not a racist, I swear. My ex is Latino. *(A short beat. She smiles nervously.)* I'm sorry. I talk too much. I say too much dumb stuff. And I forced that toothbrush on you. I'm working on it, but it's… The deodorant aisle is that way. *(She points.)* Two aisles down.

(They stare in the direction she's pointing. A short beat. A loudspeaker calls her to clean-up in another aisle.)

SUSIE. Ugh. I have to go. It was nice helping you.

MONTY. Thank you. For your help.

SUSIE. Anytime. Good luck with your deodorant!

(SUSIE exits. A beat.)

(MONTY takes a step forward, then freezes in place, clutching the toothbrush tight.)

Scene 4

(The counter of a doggy day care. A chorus of barking and yapping and yipping echoes through the walls. **MONTY** *sits at a desk filling out paperwork. The door opens and* **WARREN** *enters wearing a dirty uniform. He closes the door behind him and exhales sharply.)*

WARREN. Damn.

(short beat)

You like dogs?

MONTY. I love them.

WARREN. Yeah? Cause I'll tell you, I thought I loved dogs, too. I really did. I would see them on the street or in the park, and I would pet them and talk to them. But then I started working with them. And now I'm not so sure. Actually, I can't stand most of them. Little fuckers.

MONTY. No?

WARREN. Hell no. Dogs can be some nasty animals! Yeah, I mean, there's some nice ones, don't get me wrong, not all dogs are nasty, but dude… You ever had one bite at you? Piss on you? Shit on you? Ever had two of them gang up on you at the same time? Cause they'll do it, dude. They'll do it and not think twice.

I bet half of them are racist. I can see them thinking it. "Fucking terrorist." Most of their owners are, so I figure they must be, too. And I'm not even Arab!

MONTY. *(smiles)* No, I've never had that happen.

WARREN. Which part?

MONTY. Gang up on me. Pee or poop on me. I mean, I've been around them when they've peed or pooped,

but never, you know –   **WARREN**. On you. Welcome
on me.   to hell, my friend.

> *(He motions to the*
> *paperwork.)*

Do you mind?

MONTY. What? Oh.

> (**MONTY** *passes* **WARREN** *his resume.*)

WARREN. Seeing eye dogs?

MONTY. Yes. Service dogs, actually.

WARREN. No shit! That's wild! You trained seeing eye dogs?

MONTY. Service dogs. Yes, for a while.

WARREN. You keep correcting me.

MONTY. I'm sorry.

WARREN. I keep saying, "Seeing eye dogs," and you keep
saying, "Service dogs." What's the difference?

MONTY. Seeing eye dogs are for the blind. Service dogs
do a little bit of everything. Veterans, epileptics - a lot.
More.

WARREN. Was that your last job?

MONTY. Yes. Yes. It was.

WARREN. And you did that for the State of New York?

MONTY. Uh, yes. Yes I did.

WARREN. And how long did you do that?

MONTY. Seventeen - I mean, maybe six or seven years?

WARREN. Which was it?

MONTY. What?

WARREN. There is a very big difference between seventeen
and six or seven.

MONTY. *(referring to papers)* Actually, actually yes, it was
seven. I worked for the state for seventeen years, but I
only worked with dogs for the last seven.

WARREN. State of New York? Sweet gig. You're leaving that
for this?

MONTY. It was time.

WARREN. This is a far cry from training seeing eye dogs.

MONTY. Service dogs. Yes.

WARREN. Technically, you're overqualified.

MONTY. To work with dogs?

WARREN. I mean, here you'll mostly be cleaning up piss and shit - sometimes wet shit - feeding them, breaking up the occasional fight, and sometimes driving them home after day care.

MONTY. Driving them home?

WARREN. Yep. We chauffeur dogs here. I can't get over that. I understand the brushing and washing and feeding and all that. But chauffeuring? Like they're kids coming home from a field trip?

Our priorities are so screwed up. When you think about it, people are out there starving and these dogs are eating three course meals. You see the homeless guys outside sometimes, watching the dogs eat.

One lady brings her dog to a pet therapist. What the hell does a dog need a therapist for? They eat, sleep, shit and fight.

The shit people will waste their good money on. Let's face it, it's a fucking dog, dude. Chinese people eat dogs. Did you know that?

When I was a kid we had a yellow lab. Lived outside. Ate dry food - and take it from me? Avoid that wet stuff, dude. That wet stuff makes them shit pudding. But my dog. Didn't even need to be chained up. Came and went as he pleased. And he seemed perfectly happy - lived until he was thirteen, I think.

MONTY. Thirteen? That's old.

WARREN. Yeah. He was old. Old, yellow dog. Got rabies when he protected my mother from a wolf. So my father made me put him down myself. (*He cocks his finger like a gun.*) Pow! It was sad.

MONTY. What?

WARREN. I was just joshing. I never had a dog.

MONTY. *(relieved)* Oh.

(They laugh.)

WARREN. Anyway, this is really not a bad place to work.

(The loud yapping of a dog fight comes through the door. WARREN rises and exits.)

WARREN. *(offstage)* Abigail! Cut the shit, right now! Don't get tough with me, Miss Thing! I'll put your ass in time out! You know the drill.

(WARREN reenters, smiles sheepishly, then sits.)

WARREN. She's a nasty bitch, though. And the way she looks at me. Sometimes I half expect her to talk back to me. *(a short beat)* Do you play chess?

MONTY. Chess? A little.

WARREN. Oh. That's a Special Skill. *(He makes a note on the resume.)* I play online some times. Virtual chess. It's not the same thing as playing in person. *(off MONTY's look)* I know, I know, I'm a fucking computer geek.

MONTY. I wasn't saying that -

WARREN. Seriously, though, it does make the time fly by. Especially when it's nap time.

Anyway, if you would like, I could give you some pointers. It's not that hard and I'm really not that good. At chess, anyway. But don't test me on the Calculus, dude! I'm the LeBron James of calculus!

(He mimes a slam dunk, and smiles shyly.)

WARREN. But I don't want to force you or anything, so -

MONTY. No, no. I mean, maybe. Maybe. Does this mean I have the job?

WARREN. What job? I'm just asking you to play chess with me.

MONTY. Oh - uh - okay. Thank you.

(MONTY begins to exit.)

WARREN. When can you start?

Scene 5

(The doggy day care. **WARREN** *and* **MONTY** *play chess.*
MONTY *has his hand perched above the board, ready to
make a move.)*

WARREN. *(quiet)* That one? You going for that one? Do it.
DO IT.

*(***MONTY***'s hand moves to another piece, lingering above
it for a moment.)*

Oh…that one. Yeah, baby. Do that one. That's good
stuff.

That's what papa like. Just. Like. That.

*(***MONTY*** *pauses, sits up straight and gives* **WARREN** *a
deadpan look.* **WARREN** *stops.* **MONTY** *slowly moves a
piece across the board, his hand lingering on top of the
piece as he examines the position, then releases and sits
back.)*

WARREN. Shit. Shit! What am I gonna do now? What. Am.
I. Going. To. Do. Now?

*(He decisively moves a piece and with a fingertip knocks
Monty's queen down. Singing:)* Yeah. That's right. I took
yo' queen. I took dat bitch. Allow me to pause and cel-
ebrate this moment.

*(He stands up and begins bowing in the four directions of the
compass.)*

Black people pour out their 40's for the homies who
ain't here, my Indian brethren need to pay respect to
the four points of the compass.

MONTY. Really? Why?

WARREN. India invented the compass.

MONTY. I think China invented the compass.

WARREN. Fuck the compass and fuck China. We invented
it and they stole that shit. Who writes history? The
winners. That's why China can claim the compass.
Even though they know they stole it. We invented

badminton, the button, and chess. Which is why I whup that ass. Unfair advantage. It's in my DNA. You're much better than I thought you'd be. Hurry up and lose.

(**MONTY** *studies the board and moves a piece, taking one of* **WARREN** *'s.*)

MONTY. Check.

WARREN. Wait, what?

(**WARREN** *sits back down and stares at the board.*)

(*Loud barking from another room.* **WARREN** *glares towards the pens.*)

WARREN. Fucking Abigail. She's distracting me.

MONTY. Let me get her. She likes me.

WARREN. She tried to bite me the other day.

MONTY. She doesn't bite.

WARREN. I promise you, she does. I'd kick the bitch out but if my father found out I'd never hear the end of it.

(*More barking.* **WARREN** *studies the board.* **MONTY** *exits. A short beat. The barking ends.* **WARREN** *rises, staring through the window.* **MONTY** *reenters.*)

WARREN. How do you do that? That dog hates everyone.

MONTY. She just gets me, I guess. She hates it in there.

(**WARREN** *moves a piece.*)

WARREN. Perhaps you can help me, then. I hate it in here too.

MONTY. Weren't you supposed to be off today? Some computer thing?

WARREN. I was supposed to be at The Expo now. My friends are releasing their new computer game. It's called, "Class Dismissed."

(**MONTY** *studies the board. He moves a piece, leaning back from the table.*)

MONTY. Check mate.

WARREN. What? What are you talking about? How did you–?

(**WARREN** *studies the board. He rises, pointing a finger at* **MONTY**.)

You said you weren't good.

MONTY. No, I said I play a little.

WARREN. This sucks. All of this sucks.

(**WARREN** *crosses to the window.*)

I believe that my father hates me.

MONTY. Your father doesn't hate you.

WARREN. Why else would he do this to me? I should be presenting my new computer game today!

My friends and I started designing computer games. When I told my father, he was like, "No way, you need an industry, you need to have something solid for your future." And he bought this place and made me the manager, even though I hate dogs. And now I'm here, and my friends are making serious money designing a game where a teacher beats up bad students.

"Class Dismissed." Get it? It's a play on the word "Class," like, classroom class, and class like, the way people should behave. I came up with that. That's so awesome. It tested through the roof with schoolteachers who play computer games.

(*a short beat*)

And instead of being there, I'm here.

MONTY. It could be worse.

WARREN. Easy for you to say. Your father is not the destroyer of lives.

MONTY. My father is dead.

WARREN. I'm sorry.

MONTY. It's okay.

(*a short beat*)

WARREN. My father really is the destroyer of lives, though. That was his nickname for himself when I was a child.

I got this record - "Shamu and Friends" - for my birthday one year? It was all of the characters from "Seaworld" singing songs about the sea and about the environment. That was my shit, man - I played it over and over. And one day, my father came home in a bad mood, and I was playing it in my room and he came in and said, "Turn it down." And he closed my door, and I did, and then a few minutes later he came back in and said it again, "Turn it down." And even though I already did. And a few minutes later he came back in and grabbed the record and said, "I told you to turn that fucking thing down!" and threw it against the wall and it shattered into a million pieces. And I cried and my mother came in and was like, "Why didn't you just turn it down?" even though I did. And I wouldn't talk to him for a week, and finally a week later my mom came home with a new record and hands it to me, and it's "Sigmund the Sea Monster," which is not even nearly the same thing, and she's like, "This is from your father and me." And when I told her that it wasn't the same one, my father laughed and said, "I'm the destroyer of lives." Because he is.

(a short beat)

MONTY. I'm thirsty.

WARREN. Don't boss me.

MONTY. I won. And for the record, you made the bet.

WARREN. What do you want?

MONTY. An orange soda. And M&M's. Peanut.

WARREN. Fine. But be ready: I'm comin' back for round two.

*(**MONTY** nods. **WARREN** points at him faux-menacingly.)*

*(He exits. A beat. **MONTY** lifts a stack of papers and stares at the contents.)*

(He turns to the computer, stares at it for a moment, and clicks the mouse.)

(He works, shifting his gaze from the screen to the stack of papers. He leans forward, pointing his finger to the monitor.)

(He types on the keyboard. A beep.)

(He tries again. Another beep. A short beat.)

(SUSIE enters, watching as he tries again. Another beep. He slams his hand down on the keyboard in frustration.)

SUSIE. That's not going to help, you know.

MONTY. I know. I just– Wait – how did - how did you find me here?

SUSIE. I told you, I'm scary. Rahhhhhhh! And in addition to being scary, I'm also magic! I'm not really magic. I saw you through the window when I was walking by. The drugstore's only a couple of blocks away.

MONTY. Oh. Oh yeah.

SUSIE. Or maybe I'm stalking you!

(MONTY looks at her. She smiles shyly and looks away.)

MONTY. ...?

SUSIE. Okay, so I actually saw you in here a couple of days ago and wanted to say Hi but didn't want to bother you. And then today I ducked in here because this crazy homeless guy was following me.

(MONTY rises and walks to the window and peers out of it)

MONTY. Really? There's no one out there.

SUSIE. Oh! He must be gone.

I'm such a homeless guy target. You have no idea. It could be midnight in the middle of the worst snowstorm and some homeless guy would find me and ask for change.

SUSIE. *(cont.)* I used to give all of the homeless people change. I would carry change around with me specifically to give it to homeless people, because I always wondered, "What if that's Jesus?" You know, reincarnated Jesus coming back to test me or whatever.

Only, that doesn't really make any sense, when you think about it, because a) Jesus fed five thousand homeless people with two loaves of bread, so if it was Jesus he could take care of himself, and more importantly, b) pretending to be somebody else is a lie, and because lying is a sin it couldn't be Jesus, because he is a man without sin!

So now I don't give homeless people change any more.

(a short beat)

Hi!

MONTY. Hi. Are you okay?

SUSIE. Yeah. Yes. Yes I am okay.

(a short beat)

So.

MONTY. So.

SUSIE. How is the toothbrush?

MONTY. The toothbrush is fine.

SUSIE. What about the deodorant?

MONTY. I didn't– . You don't have the kind that I'm used to.

SUSIE. You said that last time about the toothbrush. Maybe you just need more expert insight from the right sales associate!

MONTY. …

SUSIE. *(whispering)* …That's me, by the way. In case you were wondering.

(MONTY *smiles. A short beat.)*

SUSIE. Can I ask you something?

MONTY. Yeah.

SUSIE. Why were you beating up the computer?

MONTY. Oh. Um. Because I. I can't get it to work.

SUSIE. What do you want it to do?

MONTY. I have to put these numbers – *(He holds up a stack of papers.)* – into this thing.

(He points to the screen.)

SUSIE. What thing is that? A program? A spreadsheet?

(He shrugs.)

May I?

(He nods. She crosses to him and leans over the desk.)

Oh! This is Quicktime. Pretty easy stuff. You've never used this before?

MONTY. No.

SUSIE. Where have you been, under a rock? Okay. So take your mouse –

(He grabs the mouse.)

Right. Now, right click, no, not left, right – good, like that – and then click there. No, not like that.

(She places her hand on top of his. He pulls his hand away suddenly.)

MONTY. Show me.

(She demonstrates.)

SUSIE. You tab to cross cells, and hard return to drop down to the next box. Or you can do it the long way and click everything, but I think that's the problem that you're running into, which is why it's making that sound.

(She glances to him, sees that he's watching her, and stands upright.)

Sorry. I'm doing it again. I don't mean to be rude – I'm sure you know how to do this for yourself.

MONTY. No, I don't. Thank you.

(She smiles and pats the keyboard.)

SUSIE. Nice computer. Nice. Niiiiiiiiccccccccceeeeeeeeee. You have to be nice to it.

(MONTY pets the computer, smiles. SUSIE laughs.)

(WARREN enters, depositing a brown paper bag on the desk. He regards SUSIE.)

WARREN. Hello, ma'am, how can I help you today?

MONTY. Sorry – she's not a customer, she's, uh –

SUSIE. I'm his friend. *(She extends her hand.)* Susie. Nice to meet you. And you are?

(They shake hands.)

WARREN. Warren. And you as well.

(a short awkward beat)

MONTY. I should probably get back to this.

SUSIE. Yeah, I should be getting back.

WARREN. Oh no, no rush, please excuse me, I have to go, um, check on the dogs. It was nice to meet you.

(WARREN exits.)

MONTY. So we're friends, huh?

SUSIE. I don't know about that.

MONTY. You don't? Oh - okay - I get it.

SUSIE. No, I mean…if I'm your friend, I should probably know your name. Which I still don't.

MONTY. Oh. Excuse me. *(He smiles shyly.)* I'm Monty.

SUSIE. Nice to meet you, Monty. I'm Susie.

(They shake hands, the contact lingering a little too long.)

Okay, friend, so I should - I have to get back.

MONTY. Yes, of course, goodbye, friend.

SUSIE. Goodbye.

MONTY. Watch out for homeless people.

SUSIE. You watch out for me!

(SUSIE exits. MONTY watches. A short beat. WARREN enters.)

WARREN. Play on, playa. She likes you.

MONTY. She's just being nice.

WARREN. Dude. She fucking likes you. Trust me on that.

MONTY. She came in here to get away from a homeless person.

WARREN. It makes sense that you worked with seeing eye dogs for so long. You're fucking blind.

MONTY. Service dogs.

WARREN. Whatever. She's cute.

MONTY. She is cute.

WARREN. A little too slim for me. I like 'em thicker than that, but she's definitely cute. And she definitely likes you. No woman initiates contact like that with a man without liking him. Unless she's a prostitute.

MONTY. She's not a prostitute.

WARREN. I wouldn't blame you.

(a short beat)

Okay, so... I have a confession.

(a short beat)

Earlier today, I was in the pens, laying out newspaper, and glanced down and saw a picture of someone who looked like you. And I started reading, and it was you.

(a short beat)

MONTY. I'm going to go clean the pens.

(**MONTY** grabs a mop and bucket and turns to exit.)

WARREN. It's okay, you were completely exonerated. I know you didn't do anything wrong. That's just...wow...you were there almost seventeen years, huh? Seventeen years in that place? For something you didn't do? Fucking DNA. You must be angry, man. I'm stuck in this place for an afternoon and I'm angry, you must be...wow.

(a short beat)

MONTY. I'm going to go clean the pens.

Scene 6

*(A supermarket. **MONTY**, clad in slacks, a shirt, and poorly-tied tie, holds a shopping basket. **SUSIE** stands alongside him, smiling widely.)*

MONTY. What?

SUSIE. Your tie is crooked.

MONTY. Yeah. Um. I don't really—

SUSIE. Do you want me to fix it for you?

MONTY. …yes?

SUSIE. Okay.

(She begins fixing his tie.)

This is a mess. I think we're going to have to start over.

(She removes his tie and giggles.)

You're so dressed up.

MONTY. I know.

SUSIE. Really dressed up for shopping. You're the best dressed man in Price Chopper.

(He places the basket on the floor.)

MONTY. I'm sorry. I don't mean to make you feel uncomfortable. We can go.

SUSIE. What? No! We're shopping! You asked me to help you shop, and we're shopping!

(She drapes the tie around his neck and jerks him in place, almost like a lasso.)

Hold still. You have to lift your neck so I can get the collar up.

*(**MONTY** lifts his neck. **SUSIE** begins tying the tie.)*

You act like you've never tied a tie before.

MONTY. I haven't.

SUSIE. You're cute.

(He looks down.)

Hold still.

(She fixes the tie and puts his collar down. They're really close. Her cell phone rings.)

(re: the phone) I'm sorry.

MONTY. It's okay.

(They smile nervously, she pats down his shoulders and they pull away. She checks her phone and frowns.)

Everything okay?

SUSIE. What? Sure. Must be a wrong number. Um. So. Why are you so dressed up to shop?

MONTY. No...I don't know.

SUSIE. Is that some sort of cultural thing? I only ask because, when I met you the first time you weren't dressed up. Is supermarket shopping different?

MONTY. I don't know.

(She studies him.)

SUSIE. Are you okay? Did I say something stupid?

MONTY. No, I'm okay. Just nervous.

SUSIE. It's okay. I'm nervous, too.

MONTY. You are?

SUSIE. Of course! All of these products to choose from, and you asking me to help you shop as opposed to shopping for you, and I'm like, what if I pick out the wrong scented "Pine-Sol"? What if he doesn't even like "Pine-Sol" and wanted "Mr. Clean" instead? Why did he ask me of all people?

MONTY. I liked your toothbrush.

SUSIE. You're sweet.

MONTY. And I figured I would like whatever you helped me to pick out today. I'm not very good at this.

SUSIE. I'm too good at this. Okay. So. What kind of shopping are we doing today? Are we doing price-conscious shopping, are we filling a few blanks here and there, what are we doing?

MONTY. I have a list.

SUSIE. Let's see it.

(*He hands her the list.*)

Oh. This is pretty easy. You didn't need me for this.

MONTY. Yes, I do.

SUSIE. If I didn't know better I might think you were trying to ask me out via all of this mystery shopping.

(**MONTY** *freezes.*)

MONTY. I'm sorry.

SUSIE. Oh no, poor thing - I didn't mean to make you feel bad. I'm just teasing.

(*a short beat*)

MONTY. I lied to you.

(*She steps back and freezes. A short beat.*)

SUSIE. (*quiet*) You lied to me?

MONTY. Yes.

SUSIE. About what?

MONTY. About this.

SUSIE. About shopping? Why?

MONTY. ...

SUSIE. Why did you lie to me?

MONTY. Warren. Told me to. Ask you out. Shopping. Like it was a date or something. He said you'd know that this was a date. I'm sorry.

(*They stare at one another. A short beat.* **MONTY** *looks away first.*)

SUSIE. Why didn't you just ask me?

MONTY. I've never - you know - uh.

SUSIE. Never what? Asked a girl out?

MONTY. I've never tied a tie. I've never gone shopping for groceries. And I've never asked a girl out.

SUSIE. Oh. That's a lot of nevers. (*a short beat*) You've never asked a girl out?

MONTY. ...

SUSIE. Monty?

MONTY. ...I just. Got out of prison. I was exonerated. After seventeen years. So that's. Why.

(SUSIE *bursts out laughing.*)

(*She stops. Stares. A short beat.*)

SUSIE. (*soft*) You're not kidding, are you.

MONTY. I'm going to go.

SUSIE. No – wait! Don't go. Just let me catch my breath.

MONTY. ...

(*a short beat*)

I should have told you. I'm sorry.

SUSIE. What are you sorry for? You're telling me now. (*a short beat*) I'm sorry for laughing. It's not funny. I was just. Surprised. I thought you were joking. (*She stares at him*) You said seventeen years?

(MONTY *nods.*)

For what?

MONTY. Rape.

SUSIE. ...

MONTY. ...

SUSIE. And you didn't do it?

MONTY. No.

SUSIE. And you were exonerated?

MONTY. Yes. By DNA.

SUSIE. Seventeen years?!?

(MONTY *nods. She regards him, sadly.*)

You were just...a baby...when that happened to you.

MONTY. ...

SUSIE. What's actually kind of funny is that you lied about this not being a date. You knew this was a date.

MONTY. Fucking Warren.

SUSIE. Fucking Warren. (*a short beat*) You've really never asked a girl out?

(MONTY shakes his head.)

SUSIE. *(cont.)* Have you ever kissed a girl before?

MONTY. ...No. Not a real kiss -

(She kisses him quickly, then pulls away.)

SUSIE. I've never been anyone's first kiss.

(She looks over his shoulder at something.)

MONTY. What?

SUSIE. Nothing.

MONTY. Are you sure you're okay?

SUSIE. Huh? Of course. I just - I thought I saw someone I knew. *(She grabs the basket and looks at the list.)* Okay. First up. Deodorant.

Scene 7

(Night. The dining room. **MONTY** *paces in front of the dining room window. One-two-three-four-five-six. Stop. Peek through the space between the shade and the window. Repeat. He does this for a long, long while. Silence, except for the creaks of the floor and the scuff of his feet on the carpet.)*

(An offstage door. Rustling. **LIZ** *enters, clad in weathered-ish work clothes. She stares at* **MONTY** *for a moment.)*

LIZ. Everything okay?

MONTY. Yes.

(She moves to set her bag on the table, which is neatly arranged with Monty's things. She finally drops the bag on the floor, slumps into a chair, closes her eyes, and sighs loudly.)

(A short beat. **MONTY** *begins to clear his things off of the table.* **LIZ** *opens her eyes.)*

LIZ. You don't have to do that. I can go upstairs. I didn't mean to interrupt you.

MONTY. You didn't.

(A short beat. Waiting.)

LIZ. Oh my God, what a long day. Thank God tomorrow is Saturday.

MONTY. It's Friday?

LIZ. Friday night, yes it is. You can always tell a Friday because the girls are crammed in the bathroom getting ready. Ugh. Barefoot in that bathroom. That bathroom's nasty.

MONTY. Ready for what?

LIZ. Clubbing? Dancing? I don't know. Wherever they go with short dresses and high heels and too much makeup.

MONTY. Why don't you don't go out?

LIZ. I was just out.

MONTY. Not work.

LIZ. Oh, I go. Not clubbing. But. To the movies. Sometimes. Shopping.

MONTY. You do?

LIZ. Yes.

MONTY. With who?

LIZ. The girls from work. And. Yeah.

MONTY. When?

LIZ. Whenever.

MONTY. I've never seen you.

LIZ. I do. Sometimes.

MONTY. When?

LIZ. I do.

MONTY. Okay.

> (She fake-glares at him. He smirks. She stares at him.)

What?

LIZ. Nothing. *(short beat)* I haven't seen you much lately. You're working all the time. How's your job?

MONTY. Good.

LIZ. You like it?

MONTY. Yes. I do.

LIZ. That's good. That's important. The other day I came by to say hi.

MONTY. You did?

> (She nods.)

LIZ. I was on my way home and thought I'd drop in to see how you were doing, how you liked it. I saw you through the window. You were busy. You looked - you were smiling.

MONTY. Why didn't you come in?

LIZ. I didn't want to bother you.

(She shrugs. He smiles. Another beat.)

MONTY. Do you like your job?

LIZ. Yeah, it's okay, yeah. Kevin is really, really good to me.

MONTY. But do you like it?

LIZ. It's fine. It's a job.

(a short beat)

MONTY. How come you're not a Dental Hygienist?

LIZ. ...Where did that come from?

MONTY. Didn't you - ? I thought. Nevermind.

*(**LIZ** shrugs.)*

No, you came to see me and you were excited because, you wanted, that's what you, you know. You wanted to be a Dental Hygienist. You did.

(She smiles, softens.)

LIZ. That was a long time ago.

MONTY. No.

(She nods.)

Not that long ago.

LIZ. I was nineteen.

MONTY. No.

LIZ. Yes, I was nineteen. I remember because it was just before Papi.

MONTY. Oh.

(A short beat. Silence.)

LIZ. Dental Hygienist. That's – that was. *(She shakes her head as if clearing it.)* Oh well. In another life.

(A short beat. She takes a breath.)

...Is there something wrong with your room?

MONTY. No.

LIZ. ...Is your bed uncomfortable?

MONTY. No.

LIZ. ...Is there anything we can do to make it better for you?

MONTY. No.

(LIZ *nods.*)

LIZ. If you wanna sleep down here, it's fine. I worry about you sleeping on the floor, but at least I want you to be comfortable.

MONTY. I don't sleep on the floor.

LIZ. Okay.

MONTY. I don't.

LIZ. Okay. You keep leaving the blankets folded in the corner, and the table is practically your nightstand, but– (*A beat. She composes herself.*) I don't understand. I'm trying to make this place better for you, you know? Make you more comfortable?

MONTY. I'm comfortable.

LIZ. I'm just saying, we can make this your bedroom, if you'd like.

MONTY. This isn't my bedroom.

LIZ. It's really not a big deal.

MONTY. This is the dining room.

LIZ. Yes. It is.

(*A short beat. Surrender.*)

Goodnight.

(*She grabs her bag and shoes and exits.*)

Scene 8

(The dining room. **MONTY** *and* **CHAP** *sit at the table.*
An envelope lies in the center.)

CHAP. She's persistent.

MONTY. It's not going to happen.

CHAP. I think you should at least hold on to it. Just in case.

MONTY. It's not gonna happen.

CHAP. You may change your mind.

(a short beat)

MONTY. No thank you. I'm good. I'm not angry, I'm not
bitter, it is what it is, but I'm not going to listen to her
cry and moan. It's all good.

CHAP. Do you really believe that?

(a short beat)

Okay, then.

MONTY. Okay.

(Staredown. A beat. **CHAP** *rises, stretches.)*

Don't forget your letter.

CHAP. It's not mine.

MONTY. Don't be like Warren. Whenever I beat him at
chess, he puts the board away and tells me to clean the
kennels.

*(***CHAP*** *raises his hands. Surrender. He sits.)*

CHAP. Let's get this straight: you would never beat me at
chess.

(The men smile.)

MONTY. So I've been seeing this girl –

CHAP. Really?

*(***MONTY*** *shrugs.)*

MONTY. We're at the movies and standing in line. And I
only have twenty bucks. Two tickets, some popcorn,
soda. Maybe some candies or something. That should
be more than enough, right?

(CHAP laughs. MONTY smiles sheepishly.)

MONTY. It's thirteen dollars to go to the movies now. A popcorn is nine-fifty. Nine dollars and fifty cents. How is a popcorn nine dollars and fifty cents?

CHAP. I don't go to the movies. I "Netflix."

(MONTY stares at him.)

You join this online site and they mail you DVD's.

MONTY. How do they know what you wanna see?

CHAP. You pick them on your computer, and they send them to you.

(MONTY stares at him.)

All in due time.

MONTY. We go to pay, and she's like, "I'll get the movies, you get the popcorn," —

CHAP. Good woman.

MONTY. — yes, she is – and I go over wait in line to buy popcorn and she comes back kind of shaky, you know, because this guy cut in front of her in line and took the last two tickets, so we have to see another movie.

CHAP. Bad etiquette. Worse than prison.

MONTY. Exactly. And I don't care, a movie is a movie is a movie. And we buy popcorn and a drink and we're walking, and the guy is typing onto his phone and he bumps into me and I drop everything on the floor. All of it.

And he walks away without saying anything.

(CHAP shakes his head in disgust.)

And I step forward. And she grabs my arm, you know. Holding me back.

Only there wasn't any reason to hold me back.

I was getting napkins. To clean up.

And she looks at me, and. I see.

She didn't want me to fight, but she wanted me to fight at the same time.

MONTY. *(cont.)* She expected something from me, because of what she knows about. Where I was. And. I couldn't even get that right. I couldn't even be the thing that she wanted me not to be.

(a short beat)

My father had this thing about standing up. About being a man. When I was a kid, a girl scratched my neck up. Really bad. Because I said that she liked some guy from "Manimal" and she didn't. And I went home, my neck all ripped out in the back, and my father asked what happened. And I told him and he looked at me and walked out of the room.

The same way she looked at me.

CHAP. So you're not a person that stands up?

MONTY. I guess not.

CHAP. I don't know if I believe that.

MONTY. I can't be something I'm not.

*(A short beat. **MONTY** slides the letter across the table.)*

CHAP. Did you take First Communion? I believe you once told me you did.

MONTY. Yes. In Second Grade.

CHAP. What do you remember about it?

MONTY. I mostly remember the suit. It was tight and it itched.

CHAP. Before my First Communion, they had us do a little practice session. They stood all of us in a line in the aisles, had us wait our turn, and then walked us one by one into the Confessional. Inside, we waited for the partition to slide, at which time we'd been instructed to say, "Forgive me, Father, for I have sinned," and then list our sins.

And when my turn came, I couldn't think of any. I was blank.

And I sat there, and waited. And waited. And waited for something to come to me. But nothing came.

CHAP. *(cont.)* And then I heard a voice - and at first I thought it was God, and that His voice was really high and soft and whiny. And after a moment I realized it was Father Patenaude, offering me some ideas. He asked me if I swore, and if I lied, and if I was mean to my sister, and whether I stole - a short laundry list of a child's sins. And I said Yes all of those things, and he gave me penance, and that was that.

And some time later, when I realized I was heading down this career path, I remembered that moment, and found it conflicting. That idea of being nudged towards confession. Of being coached. Of helping someone take their first steps towards something.

MONTY. And now you think you understand it.

CHAP. Not entirely. But I do think I can help you, Monty. I think we can help each another.

MONTY. I have nothing to confess.

CHAP. That's not what I'm talking about.

MONTY. And I don't need your nudging.

(a short beat)

Why do you keep pushing this on me? You keep trying to make me go back to this, man. Let it fucking go, I just want to let it go—

CHAP. No, I'm not. That's not what this is about. I'm trying to help you.

MONTY. You mean you, right? *You're* trying to help *you.* This isn't about me don't use me. Call it what it is! You feel like shit because you didn't believe me. You got it wrong. And maybe that means that you got something else - someone else - wrong, too. And so by trying to make me talk to her, or whatever, *she* feels better and *you* feel better. Isn't that right?

CHAP. ...

MONTY. You're trying to, absolve yourself of your own sins.

CHAP. This is not about my absolution.

MONTY. You want me to let both of you off the hook for your fuck-ups. And I'll tell you right fucking now -

CHAP. Look, Monty - you got a bad deal. It happens to people all of the time. And this is not - it can not be - about that anymore.

MONTY. What happened to me does not happen to other people.

CHAP. The point is it happened. It's done. You can't go back. You can't undo any of the horrible shit that happened to you. No one can do a thing about any of it.

The question is: What do you want to do now?

You can quit going to your cell, brother.

Scene 9

*(The doggy day care. **MONTY** sits at the desk, working. He's faster now. **WARREN** enters, staring at **MONTY**. A short beat.)*

WARREN. Wanna play chess?

MONTY. No.

WARREN. Wanna clean up some dog pee?

*(**MONTY** rises)*

MONTY. Which kennel?

WARREN. None. I was just asking you if you wanted to clean up some dog pee, not that there was any dog pee to clean up.

*(**MONTY** sits and resumes his work.)*

So my friends were approached by a major gaming company after the Expo.

*(**MONTY** works. A short beat. Silence.)*

They sold the game for mucho dinero.

*(**MONTY** works. A short beat. Silence.)*

Right this moment, they are in a fancy-pants meeting signing contracts. And I am here, swimming in the fumes of canine urine with an employee who refuses to play chess with - or speak to - me.

*(**MONTY** works. A short beat. Silence.)*

Are you still angry because I told you to dress up for your shopping date? Dude, that was forever ago! A gentleman always wears a tie.

*(**MONTY** works. A short beat. **WARREN** crosses to the desk.)*

What are you working on? The billing sheet, still? I thought you were done with that.

(a short beat)

Monty? I thought you were done with all of that?

MONTY. I'm just double-checking it.

WARREN. You're very thorough.

MONTY. It's my job.

WARREN. You're a good employee, Monty. You are always on time, you always do as you're told, and you're always ready for your next task. And your next task is to play chess with me.

(Silence. WARREN crosses, grabs the chessboard, and sets it up.)

C'mon, man. Let's play. I can beat you this time.

(MONTY works. A short beat. Silence.)

Why are you angry with me?

(MONTY stops working and looks up.)

MONTY. Because you don't do that, man. You do not fucking do that.

(He points towards the kennels.)

WARREN. Abigail tried to bite me.

MONTY. She did not try to bite you, Warren. I was there. She didn't so much as lunge at you.

WARREN. She tried to bite me -

MONTY. No, she did not. I saw everything. And you just – you kicked her.

WARREN. She tried to bite me.

MONTY. It doesn't matter, Warren! You don't fucking do that! You don't kick a dog! You don't hurt a dog! You don't scream at a dog!

(a short beat)

WARREN. I hate this place.

MONTY. I understand that.

WARREN. It's like prison.

MONTY. No it's not.

(a short beat)

MONTY. *(cont.)* She's locked in there because her fucking owners are too fucking busy to take care of her and fucking pay for us to be her nannies. It's not her fault, man.

WARREN. It does not excuse her behavior.

MONTY. She's reacting off of-of-of instinct. Off of what she gets off of you! You go in there excited, nervous, angry, she's gonna react to that. You can't go in there swinging big dick.

(A staredown. A long beat.)

You're Indian. Like Gandhi. Aren't you supposed to be all Buddhist or Hindu, non-violence as a means to an end?

WARREN. My family is Old-Testament Catholic.

MONTY. Oooh. That's no good.

*(**MONTY** stares at **WARREN**. A short beat.)*

WARREN. This is not what I want.

*(**MONTY** sits down at the chess board.)*

MONTY. C'mon, man. Your move.

Scene 10

(Susie's bedroom. She sits on the edge of the bed, her head hanging. **MONTY** *sits in the middle of the bed, shirtless, the sheets gathered up around him. Silence, then:)*

SUSIE. Is it me?

(a short beat)

MONTY. No.

(a short beat)

SUSIE. Is it you?

(a short beat)

MONTY. ...

(a short beat)

SUSIE. It's me, isn't it.

(a short beat)

MONTY. No.

(a short beat)

SUSIE. Did I do something wrong?

(a short beat)

MONTY. ...

(a short beat)

SUSIE. Is there something that I'm not doing right?

(a short beat)

MONTY. ...

(a short beat)

SUSIE. Is it because I wouldn't take my shirt off?

(a short beat)

MONTY. No.

(a short beat)

SUSIE. Could you maybe give me a little bit more than the one- syllable answers? It's not a lot to play with.

MONTY. ...

SUSIE. I don't understand.

MONTY. ...

SUSIE. I really don't understand what's wrong with me.

MONTY. There's nothing wrong with you.

(a longer beat)

SUSIE. This isn't the first time this has happened to me, Monty. This used to happen with Eddie, too.

(a short beat)

SUSIE. Yes. Eddie, Ex, Eddie.

Fucking psychopath, won't stop showing up at my work, Eddie. It wasn't as abrupt as this – because, you know, from my experience – not that I'm super experienced or anything – but you're supposed to just go crazy on each other your first time.

I did with Eddie, anyway. At first.

And it was usually okay because the sex was okay, and I figured that if the sex was okay, that must mean that I was good enough, you know?

And then that started to get bad, and he would blame me for it and – and then it got worse. Much worse. I would try to help him and he would call me bossy. I would ask how his day was and he would tell me to shut the fuck up because I talk too much.

And then:

(She lifts her shirt and closes her eyes. Her midsection is covered in scarred-over bite marks. MONTY stares.)

They're teeth marks.

Bite marks.

It looks awful, right? It didn't feel that awful. It didn't feel as awful as this.

(A short beat. She lowers her shirt.)

SUSIE. *(cont.)* I'm tired of feeling like this, you know? Dirty. Ruined. Like I stink or like I'm I'm I'm defective or like I'm, whatever, repulsive or something. I feel like, like I could shower in boiling hot water with tons of soap and be super clean and it wouldn't matter, I would still be dirty and smelly and everything I do would still be wrong. I want to feel clean.

(a long beat)

MONTY. I'm sorry.

SUSIE. It's not about sorry, Monty! I don't want you to be sorry! I want you to do something. Be a man! Man the fuck up and either take me or leave me but don't do this, this in between shit.

(She crosses to the center of the room and turns to him.)

I thought ex-cons were like, ravenous or something? I mean, I know you were cleared of everything, but still, isn't that how you're supposed to be?

(She exits.)

Scene 11

(The dining room. **CHAP** *and* **LIZ** *sit at the table.* **MONTY** *enters, pauses. They rise.)*

LIZ. Hey Mont.

CHAP. How are you, good sir?

MONTY. Fine.

(They shake hands.)

LIZ. Late night, huh?

*(***MONTY*** looks away.)*

LIZ. Well then. Monty? Can I get you anything? *(to* **CHAP***)* More tea?

MONTY. No.

CHAP. Please.

(She winks at him.)

LIZ. Great.

(She exits. **CHAP** *gestures to the table.)*

CHAP. Mind if we sit?

MONTY. You asking me or telling me?

CHAP. We should sit.

(They sit.)

MONTY. This feels official.

CHAP. We have a few things to discuss.

MONTY. Heh.

CHAP. Well then. First. The good news.

MONTY. That means there's bad news.

CHAP. Not necessarily.

MONTY. Start with the bad news. If you start with the bad news, the good news might make it a wash. Bad news first, please.

*(***LIZ*** reenters with tea.)*

CHAP. *(to* **LIZ***)* Thank you.

LIZ. Should I go?

CHAP. That might be

best.   **MONTY**. No, it's fine. Sit.
                                        You'll find out anyway.

(She sits.)

CHAP. Let's start with this: Laura Miller.

MONTY. *(a small laugh)*

*(**LIZ** sits up uncomfortably straight.)*

CHAP. Formally reached out to us. Again. Asked if we could
      help broker a conversation with you. She wants to talk.

LIZ. She wants to apologize.

CHAP. Yes, that's certainly
      part of it. Although
      I think—   **LIZ**. Too late. Fuck her.

MONTY. She doesn't want to apologize, she wants to make
      herself feel better, is what she wants. Isn't that right,
      Chap?

CHAP. That may well be.

      But as I—   **LIZ**. Fuck. Her.

MONTY. Liz.

(He rises and paces.)

(snapping his fingers) Next. What's next.

CHAP. Do you want to sit?

MONTY. No, I don't want to sit. I want you to tell me what's
      next.

CHAP. Very well.

      Ripley.

*(**MONTY** stops.)*

MONTY. Ripley what?

(a short beat)

What about her?

CHAP. ...Is gone.

MONTY. She's gone?

CHAP. Yes.

MONTY. What do you mean, gone?

CHAP. There was an accident. A car—

LIZ. Oh, Monty.

CHAP. She's gone.

MONTY. When? When did this happen?

CHAP. I don't know. I just learned about this myself. Wojo—

...I'm so sorry.

(**MONTY** *crosses to the table and sits, hands clasped in front of him.*)

(*a long beat*)

MONTY. What's next?

CHAP. I know what she   LIZ. Monty...
meant to you, and –

MONTY. (*interrupting*) What's next?

CHAP. Please, Monty. I would like to take a moment -

MONTY. What. Is. Next. What's next?!? The good news! What is the fucking good news? What is fucking next?

(*a short beat*)

CHAP. The State is beginning to formally process your re-compensation. You haven't returned any of their messages, so I've been asked to relay some of this to you.

MONTY. ...

CHAP. Looks like it will be around $250,000.

MONTY. Okay.

CHAP. You could hire a lawyer, of course, and could probably get a great deal more — New York State has no compensation limits — but that will probably take a much longer amount of time.

LIZ. We'll hire a lawyer.

CHAP. That's totally understandable.

MONTY. No, we won't.

LIZ. We will, Monty. That's, like what, not even fifteen thousand a year? Fuck that. We'll hire a lawyer. We've gone this long, we can—

MONTY. *(cutting her off)* No we won't.
I already talked to   **LIZ**. Monty, we should —
them. I told them.

LIZ. Wait, what? Who did you talk to?

MONTY. *(to CHAP)* I already talked to them. I don't know why they're coming to you. They shouldn't have done that. Nothing has changed. I just want all of this over with.

LIZ. Monty - *who did you talk to?*

MONTY. *(sharp)* Liz.

LIZ. Why would you do that?

> (**MONTY** *rises, extending his hand to* **CHAP**).

MONTY. Tell them I— . Thank you.

LIZ. The two of us need to talk about this, Monty — they owe you. They owe us.

MONTY. Please shut up, Liz.

LIZ. What? Don't tell me that—

MONTY. Please shut up and mind your business.

LIZ. I'm just looking out for you, Monty—

MONTY. This isn't about us.

LIZ. This isn't just about you.   **MONTY**. Shut the fuck up, Liz! Shut up!

> (**LIZ** *rises. Fury.*)

LIZ. Don't you tell me to shut the fuck up! You shut the fuck up!

MONTY. This has nothing to do with you! This is not yours to take!

LIZ. This has everything to do with me! What, you think you think you did your time in a-a-a, a fuckin' vacuum? You think you did it alone? Who do you think held all of this shit down? I did seventeen with you, mothafuckah!

(CHAP rises and puts his arm on her shoulder.)

CHAP. You should go. For a few moments. We can talk after.

LIZ. *(seething)* Fuck you.

(Staredown. A beat. She exits.)

CHAP. You shouldn't take this out on Liz. It's not her fault.

(a long beat)

MONTY. Ripley was a good dog, man.

CHAP. She was.

MONTY. A good dog. No, a great fucking dog. The best. I taught her to sit. I taught her to stay. I taught her to lie down. I taught her to shake - even though I wasn't supposed to. I taught her to nudge someone's hand when they were scared or angry or anxious or just, just shut the fuck down. Me. I did that.

The first night in that place with me, she cried. She fucking whined, man. Just scared. Cold and dark and metal and concrete and fucking...hell, man. Fucking hell. And because I was used to it, I had to make her okay. And I got down on the floor with her, on her bed, and laid down next to her, and I talked to her all night and stroked her head - that was her favorite - the top of her head - and took care of her. I made her not afraid. I made her okay. I did that. I got her through hell and I made something good happen. One good thing that I did.

MONTY. *(cont.)* And now it's like everything else. Gone, man. It's all gone.

I have nothing.

(a long beat)

Laura Miller can suck my dick. Fuck that bitch, man. Fuck her.

The state can suck my dick. $250,000? $10 mill? What's the fucking difference, man?

I am seventeen years old. Seven-fucking-teen.

I don't know how to tie a tie.

I don't know how to shop for toothbrushes or deodorant or toilet paper.

I don't know how to use a computer.

I don't know how to kiss.

My dick doesn't work.

I can't help my friend, I can't protect a woman.

I cannot do anything anything ANYTHING without being told to.

The only fucking good thing I ever did is gone, and you come here telling me that the good news is that they want to pay me for missing my prom and college and keg parties and my first apartment?

Fuck them.

Fuck the dude that killed my dog.

And fuck Laura Miller.

(A long beat. He turns to the window.)

Show yourself out, man.

(A long beat. CHAP rises and exits.)

Scene 12

(The dining room. MONTY sits at the table. LIZ enters, holding a cup of tea. She watches him. A beat.)

LIZ. You want to sleep? I can leave.

MONTY. No.

LIZ. Can I sit?

MONTY. No.

(MONTY sits. LIZ glowers at him. A beat.)

LIZ. Don't ever say that to me again. Don't ever tell me "Shut the fuck up" again, you understand me? I don't talk to you like that, you don't talk to me like that.

MONTY. ...

LIZ. And you don't ever remove me from decisions that directly affect me, or this family.

MONTY. It's not your money, Liz.

LIZ. I know it's not my money. That's not the point. You need to do something with that money, to take it for *you.* I don't want your money -

MONTY. Sounds like it.

(She slams her hands down on the table.)

LIZ. Don't you be smart don't you dare be smart! If you're going to live here, and we're going to try to pretend to be a normal fucking family, you at least owe me a conversation about it! That's what families do! Families talk to each other and listen to each other and take each other in-in-into consid*eration!*

MONTY. Okay.

LIZ. It's not okay! It's not okay it's not okay it's not okay! None of this is okay!

(LIZ slumps into a chair. A short beat.)

MONTY. ...We're not normal.

We're never going to be normal, Liz.

LIZ. We can't even at least fucking try?

MONTY. …

LIZ. Talk to me, Monty.

MONTY. …

LIZ. When Chap comes here? You talk to *him*. I stand on the other side of the door, and lean against the wall, and listen to what you talk about. Or yell about. Or laugh about.

   (**MONTY** *stares at her.*)

About you playing chess at work, and how your suit itched at First Communion, and when Sammy Day scratched your neck at school, and how you can't walk at the street lights.

And today, how you have nothing.

And I don't understand that. Because you have a roof over your head. A home. And you have a job that you really like. And you have a girl to go to the movies with. And you have your freedom.

And you have me.

And I'm like, "That's nothing? Really? That's nothing?"

Because it doesn't sound like nothing.

I would trade for that.

   (*She stares at him.*)

MONTY. …

LIZ. I feel like I'm all by myself. Still. And it shouldn't be like that anymore.

   (*She stares at him, waiting. He stares back at her.*)

   (*She rises and exits.*)

Scene 13

*(The doggy day care. **EDDIE** stands near the counter, waiting. A beat. [Over the course of this scene, the barking should slowly and steadily increase.])*

MONTY. *(offstage)* I'll be right with you!

*(Silence. **EDDIE** waits. **MONTY** enters.)*

Sorry about that. The dogs are going crazy in there. Can I help you?

EDDIE. This is a nice place.

MONTY. Thank you.

EDDIE. You been here a long time?

MONTY. The store? Uh - I think that the store is maybe a couple of years old.

EDDIE. No, you. You been here a long time?

MONTY. A month.

EDDIE. Oh. Huh. Well, I'm looking for something to help discipline my dog. Do you have anything like that?

MONTY. Depends on what you're looking for. What problems are you having?

EDDIE. Oh. Um. Just an all around bad dog.

MONTY. Does she chew -

EDDIE. He.

MONTY. Okay. What kind of bad dog is he? Does he chew on things, pee on the floor, is he aggressive -

EDDIE. He doesn't really listen. He takes things that don't belong to him.

*(He stares at **MONTY**.)*

Don't I know you?

MONTY. Me? No. I don't think so.

EDDIE. Are you sure? Because you look pretty familiar.

MONTY. I don't think that we've met.

EDDIE. Huh. Oh well. So. My bad dog. What do you recommend?

MONTY. For obedience, there are gentle leaders, harnesses, choke chains — for the bigger dogs —

EDDIE. Do you have any shock collars?

MONTY. Shock collars? No, we don't carry those.

EDDIE. I've heard that those work.

MONTY. I wouldn't know. I've never used one.

EDDIE. You've never used one?

MONTY. I - uh - no.

EDDIE. *(chuckling)* You're one of those.

MONTY. One of what?

EDDIE. One of those humane dog lovers.

MONTY. Yes, I guess I am.

(**EDDIE** *walks behind the counter.*)

EDDIE. How do you keep your dog in line, then?

MONTY. I don't have a dog.

EDDIE. You don't?

MONTY. No, I don't.

EDDIE. Huh. Here you are, working in a dog shop, but you don't have a dog. You sure you don't have a dog?

MONTY. Yes. I mean, no, I don't have a dog.

(**EDDIE** *stares at him.*)

EDDIE. You sure I don't know you?

MONTY. I don't think so.

EDDIE. *(snapping his fingers)* I know who you are! You're the guy that likes to fuck other guy's girls.

MONTY. Girls? What– ? *(a realization)* Susie?

(**EDDIE** *punches him in the face.*)

(**MONTY** *falls to the floor. He recovers and begins crawling away.*)

EDDIE. Keep her name outta your mouth! She called me, crying. She came back to me, crying!

(**MONTY** *stands.* **EDDIE** *punches him again in the ribs.*)

EDDIE. Stay down, bitch! Stay down!

> (**MONTY** *stands.*)

STAY DOWN, MOTHAFUCKAH!

> (**EDDIE** *kicks him in the side, knocking him back to the floor.*)

> (*He spits on* **MONTY**.)

Keep your ass down!

> (**EDDIE** *moves to exit.*)

> (**MONTY** *stands.*)

> (*A decision. He races forward and tackles* **EDDIE** *into the wall.*)

> (*They fight.* **EDDIE** *finally beats* **MONTY** *down.*)

Shoulda kept your ass down.

> (**EDDIE** *exits.*)

> (*The door dings.*)

> (*The dogs bark, louder and louder, building to a crescendo.*)

> (*blackout*)

Scene 14

(The dining room. **WARREN** *sits at the table, a chess board in front of him.* **LIZ** *stands in the doorway, dolled up and adjusting her earrings.)*

LIZ. Where's Monty?

WARREN. In the bathroom. Do you think he's peeing blood? In sixth grade I got hit in the back with a soft-ball and I peed blood.

LIZ. I...really don't know. I hope not.

WARREN. Probably not anymore. You usually pee blood right afterwards. It doesn't really hurt, it just looks weird.

(He stares at her. A short beat.)

LIZ. Can I get you anything?

WARREN. No, thank you.

(a short beat)

So you look nice.

LIZ. Thank you.

*(***WARREN*** *stares.)*

It's really nice of you to come by to see him. He's home alone, most of the time, so—. It's nice of you.

WARREN. He calls to check on the dogs. But I haven't seen him in two weeks and we both wanted to play chess, so...

*(***MONTY*** *enters, walking slowly. He stops, stares at* **LIZ**.*)*

MONTY. *(to* **LIZ***)* Where are you going?

LIZ. Out.

MONTY. Out where?

LIZ. Out. For the weekend.

MONTY. With who?

LIZ. A friend.

MONTY. When will you be back?

LIZ. When I'm back. Monday, maybe. Bye.

WARREN. Bye!

MONTY. Bye.

> *(She exits.* MONTY *turns back to the game.* WARREN *stares at the door.* MONTY *snaps his fingers at him. A short beat.)*

WARREN. Dude, I can't believe you live in the dining room.

MONTY. Easier for me to get around the house.

WARREN. It's your move.

MONTY. I'm thinking.

WARREN. You're stalling. Because I'm winning. ...So she's cute.

MONTY. She's my sister.

WARREN. I'll play you for her.

MONTY. I'll lose on purpose.

> *(*MONTY *stares at the board.)*

WARREN. So...I spoke to my father.

MONTY. And?

WARREN. He was not happy with me.

MONTY. Oh.

WARREN. So I spoke to him again.

MONTY. And?

WARREN. He was not happy with me.

MONTY. Oh.

WARREN. So I spoke to him again.

MONTY. Jesus, Warren -

WARREN. And he was not happy with me, but he said "Maybe."

MONTY. Maybe?

WARREN. Yes. Maybe. And you have to understand, it's the first time he's ever said maybe, so, you may soon be a partner in the glamorous world of doggy day care. And I will be the serious money guy, lurking in the shadows, twirling my moustache.

(MONTY sits up straight, excited, wincing as he does. He places his hand over his ribs.)

MONTY. Ahhhhh...

WARREN. That's the most excited I've ever seen you.

MONTY. I have to warn you. The money will take a while to come through.

WARREN. So will my father. And until he does you can continue to clean up dog piss.

(MONTY stares at the board.)

WARREN. Make your move.

(MONTY stares at him.)

Don't menace me. I refuse to be intimidated.

(SUSIE enters.)

MONTY. *(surprised)* Hi.

WARREN. Hi.

SUSIE. Hi. Your sister let me in. Is this a bad time?

MONTY. No.

(WARREN sets down the game and stares at the board.)

WARREN. Make your move.

(MONTY stares at WARREN)

WARREN. Oh. Um. If you'll excuse me for a moment... *(to SUSIE)* Can I trust you to watch the game for me?

SUSIE. Yeah, sure.

WARREN. It's important. We're playing for Monty's sister.

(WARREN exits. SUSIE moves one of the pieces.)

MONTY. He's going to notice that.

SUSIE. Hi.

MONTY. *(studying chessboard)* Hi. This is a nice surprise.

SUSIE. I wanted to see how you are.

MONTY. Okay.

SUSIE. How are you?

MONTY. I'm fine.

SUSIE. You look fine.

MONTY. I have three broken ribs and a punctured lung, but I should be able to go back to work in a week or so.

(a short beat)

SUSIE. I quit the drug store.

MONTY. ...What are you going to do?

SUSIE. Go back to school, maybe. Yeah right. I'll probably end up working at another drug store.

MONTY. What do you want to do?

SUSIE. I have no idea.

MONTY. What do you like to do?

SUSIE. I have no idea.

MONTY. You're good at scaring people.

SUSIE. I am good at that! Rahhhhhhh!

MONTY. And helping pick out toothbrushes.

SUSIE. I could be a personal shopper.

MONTY. I'd hire you.

(She looks at him, sadly, lifts his hand and kisses it. A short beat.)

SUSIE. I don't think I can see you for a little while.

MONTY. I know.

SUSIE. I just. After what happened...what I did. I just need to—

I'm going to stay with my sister. And—. Think.

Awesome, right?

I'm sorry, Monty. I can't believe that Eddie...

(She stares at him.)

MONTY. ...

(He kisses her hand. A long beat. She weeps, silently.)

SUSIE. This hurts so bad. I mean, I haven't even known you that long, but it just, doing this feels… Even though I know it's right, I know that I'm supposed to do this, to take care of me, to get myself together, it hurts so bad.

I convinced myself, I'll see him, we'll smile, we'll say goodbye, and that will be it. But I see you sitting here, now, and it's So. Hard. I'm terrified that I'm going to walk out of here and have regrets, you know? That in a day or a hundred days or a thousand days I'll still regret it.

(a beat)

MONTY. Did you know that my father wouldn't go to my trial?

SUSIE. No, I didn't.

MONTY. Mom and Liz did, but he refused. I'm the only boy, the one who was supposed to carry on the family name, and I ruined it for him.

SUSIE. What about your mom?

MONTY. Mothers always believe you're innocent, that something that came out of them is good. Fathers always believe you're guilty, that something that came out of the mother can't be their fault. She knew I didn't do it. And even though she passed before she found out for sure, she knew. She could see it.

But my father wouldn't even look. My father died thinking that his boy—his only son—was a rapist.

(a short beat)

So this? Is nothing. You do you. You handle what you have to handle.

(a short beat)

And when—if—you're ready? You know where to find me.

(He kisses her hand.)

(The phone rings offstage.)

MONTY. *(calling)* Could you get that, Warren?

WARREN. *(offstage)* Sho' nuff!

(a short beat)

MONTY. I hope I see you again.

SUSIE. You will.

MONTY. I hope so.

(They kiss. A short, sweet, wonderful kiss.)

(WARREN enters, immediately shielding his eyes.)

WARREN. You have a phone call, Monty.

SUSIE. I was just leaving.

MONTY. Goodbye.

*(She crosses, **MONTY** walks alongside her, stopping in the center of the room.)*

(She stops at the door.)

SUSIE. Rahhhh!

(She exits. He watches her depart.)

WARREN. You want to take this?

MONTY. *(still looking after her)* Who is it?

WARREN. *(into phone)* May I ask who's speaking? *(to **MONTY**)* Laura Miller?

*(A long, long beat. **MONTY** stares ahead.)*

*(As he stares, lights fade on **WARREN**, leaving **MONTY** surrounded by blackness.)*

(Lights rise, flare, bathing him in light, almost blindingly.)

(As he turns towards the light–)

(blackout)

End of Play

OTHER TITLES AVAILABLE FROM SAMUEL FRENCH

A BRIGHT NEW BOISE

Samuel D. Hunter

Comedy / 3m, 2f / Interior

Winner! 2011 Obie Award for Playwriting
Nominated for the 2011 Drama Desk Award for Outstanding Play

Samuel D. Hunter's *A Bright New Boise* is a earnest comedy about the meager profits of modern faith.

In the bleak, corporate break room of a craft store in Idaho, someone is summoning The Rapture. Will, who has fled his rural hometown after a scandal at his Evangelical church, comes to the Hobby Lobby, not only for employment, but also to rekindle a relationship with Alex, his brooding teenage son, whom he gave up for adoption several years ago. Alex works there along with Leroy, his adopted brother and protector, and Anna, a hapless young woman who reads bland fiction but hopes for dramatic endings. As their manager, foul-mouthed Pauline, tries ceaselessly to find order (and profit) in the chaos of small business, these lost souls of the Hobby Lobby confront an unyielding world through the beige-tinted impossibility of modern faith.

"Nothing is pretty about *A Bright New Boise*, a play that marches in the footsteps of Sam Shepard's acid comedies, set in the weird American West...Hunter has such highly sensitive antennae for the look and rhythm of mundane places that *A Bright New Boise* develops an authentic texture, separate from other pieces in its genre."
– *The Washington Post*

"This clear-eyed comedy will lift your heart."
– *Time Out New York*

SAMUELFRENCH.COM

OTHER TITLES AVAILABLE FROM SAMUEL FRENCH

THE SECRET LIVES OF LOSERS

Megan Mostyn-Brown

Drama / 2w, 3m, 1 female voiceover / Multiple Sets

In high school, Neely was deemed "Most Likely to Succeed," but at 19, she's still working at the Amoco station and taking care of her meth-addicted younger brother (their mom ran out on them in search of herself). Her best-friend is a small-time drug dealer (also 19) who's taking care of the baby he had with a girl who has gone off to college abandoning them both. Into this mess strolls a new cop, who takes an interest in Neely and starts to date her. A swift-moving, compassionate script about young adults in bad circumstances looking for a way out.

OTHER TITLES AVAILABLE FROM SAMUEL FRENCH

TOMORROWLAND

Neena Beber

Comedy / 3m, 4f / Multiple Sets

Anna has left graduate school to join the real world, as a writer on a children's television show in Orlando, Florida, she finds that world to be more surreal and absurd than anything she's left behind. *Tomorrowland* takes a darkly comic look at death, Disney, and the search for meaning in a world that worships the young and the fake.

"Briskly hilarious comedy about a brittle New Yorker who abandons her doctoral dissertation on Virginia Woolf's use of parenthesis to write scripts for kid's TV show."
– *Washington City Paper*

"If you are not already terrified by the prospect of the Disneyfication of America, this wry exploration of its possible effects will put the fear of Mickey in you."
– *Time Out*

SAMUEL FRENCH STAFF

Nate Collins
President

Ken Dingledine	**Bruce Lazarus**	**Rita Maté**
Director of Operations,	Executive Director,	Director of Finance
Vice President	General Counsel	

ACCOUNTING

Lori Thimsen | Director of Licensing Compliance
Nehal Kumar | Senior Accounting Associate
Josephine Messina | Accounts Payable
Helena Mezzina | Royalty Administration
Joe Garner | Royalty Administration
Jessica Zheng | Accounts Receivable
Andy Lian | Accounts Receivable
Zoe Qiu | Accounts Receivable
Charlie Sou | Accounting Associate
Joann Mannello | Orders Administrator

BUSINESS AFFAIRS

Lysna Marzani | Director of Business Affairs
Kathryn McCumber | Business Administrator

CUSTOMER SERVICE AND LICENSING

Brad Lohrenz | Director of Licensing Development
Fred Schnitzer | Business Development Manager
Laura Lindson | Licensing Services Manager
Kim Rogers | Professional Licensing Associate
Matthew Akers | Amateur Licensing Associate
Ashley Byrne | Amateur Licensing Associate
Glenn Halcomb | Amateur Licensing Associate
Derek Hassler | Amateur Licensing Associate
Jennifer Carter | Amateur Licensing Associate
Kelly McCready | Amateur Licensing Associate
Annette Storckman | Amateur Licensing Associate
Chris Lonstrup | Outgoing Information Specialist

EDITORIAL AND PUBLICATIONS

Amy Rose Marsh | Literary Manager
Ben Coleman | Editorial Associate
Gene Sweeney | Graphic Designer
David Geer | Publications Supervisor
Charlyn Brea | Publications Associate
Tyler Mullen | Publications Associate

MARKETING

Abbie Van Nostrand | Director of Corporate Communications
Ryan Pointer | Marketing Manager
Courtney Kochuba | Marketing Associate

OPERATIONS

Joe Ferreira | Product Development Manager
Casey McLain | Operations Supervisor
Danielle Heckman | Office Coordinator, Reception

SAMUEL FRENCH BOOKSHOP (LOS ANGELES)

Joyce Mehess | Bookstore Manager
Cory DeLair | Bookstore Buyer
Jennifer Palumbo | Customer Service Associate
Sonya Wallace | Bookstore Associate
Tim Coultas | Bookstore Associate
Monté Patterson | Bookstore Associate
Robin Hushbeck | Bookstore Associate
Alfred Contreras | Shipping & Receiving

LONDON OFFICE

Felicity Barks | Rights & Contracts Associate
Steve Blacker | Bookshop Associate
David Bray | Customer Services Associate
Zena Choi | Professional Licensing Associate
Robert Cooke | Assistant Buyer
Stephanie Dawson | Amateur Licensing Associate
Simon Ellison | Retail Sales Manager
Jason Felix | Royalty Administration
Susan Griffiths | Amateur Licensing Associate
Robert Hamilton | Amateur Licensing Associate
Lucy Hume | Publications Manager
Nasir Khan | Management Accountant
Simon Magniti | Royalty Administration
Louise Mappley | Amateur Licensing Associate
James Nicolau | Despatch Associate
Martin Phillips | Librarian
Zubayed Rahman | Despatch Associate
Steve Sanderson | Royalty Administration Supervisor
Douglas Schatz | Acting Executive Director
Roger Sheppard | I.T. Manager
Geoffrey Skinner | Company Accountant
Peter Smith | Amateur Licensing Associate
Garry Spratley | Customer Service Manager
David Webster | UK Operations Director

SAMUELFRENCH.COM
SAMUELFRENCH-LONDON.CO.UK